CRITT[ER] KITTY-CAM

Meow!

written by
MARGIE PALATINI

illustrated by
DAN YACCARINO

Ready-to-Read

SIMON SPOTLIGHT

New York London Toronto Sydney New Delhi

For Jack, My Little Pup
—M. P.

To our family cat who was named after my uncle.
(Don't ask.)
—D. Y.

SIMON SPOTLIGHT
An imprint of Simon & Schuster Children's Publishing Division
1230 Avenue of the Americas, New York, New York 10020
This Simon Spotlight edition June 2023
Text copyright © 2023 by Margie Palatini
Illustrations copyright © 2023 by Dan Yaccarino
For information about special discounts for bulk purchases, please contact Simon & Schuster Specials Sales at
1-866-506-1949 or business@simonandschuster.com.
Manufactured in the United States of America 0723 LAK
2 4 6 8 10 9 7 5 3
This book has been cataloged with the Library of Congress.
ISBN 978-1-6659-2732-1 (hc)
ISBN 978-1-6659-2731-4 (pbk)
ISBN 978-1-6659-2733-8 (ebook)

Jump, Kitty.
Jump. Jump. Jump.

Dunk, Kitty. Dunk.

WET!

RECORD

Shake.

Shake.

Shake.

RECORD

Yum!

RECORD

Yum! Yum! Yum! Yum!

Wash chin,
wash whiskers,
wash nose and toes.

Yawn.

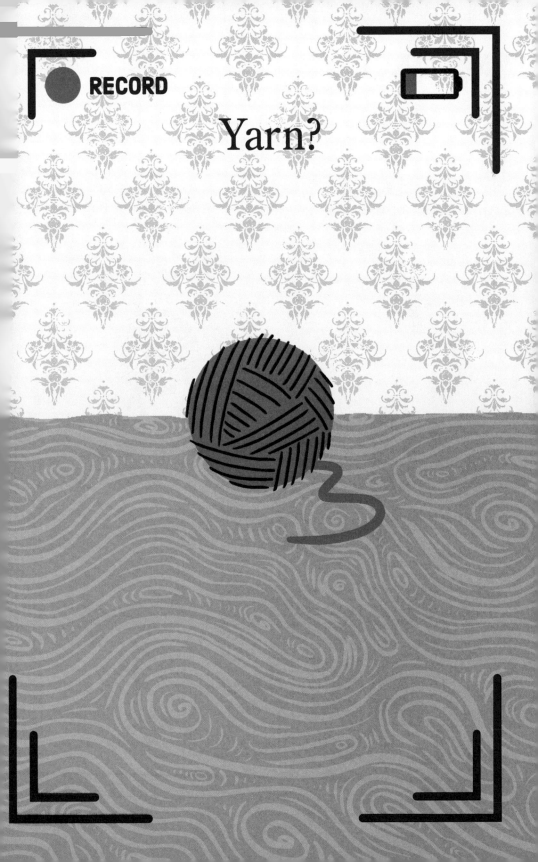

Yarn?

YARN!

Yarn. Yarn. Yarn. Yarn. Yarn. Yarn. Yarn.

Wait. Wait. Wait.
Wait. Wait. Wait. Wait.

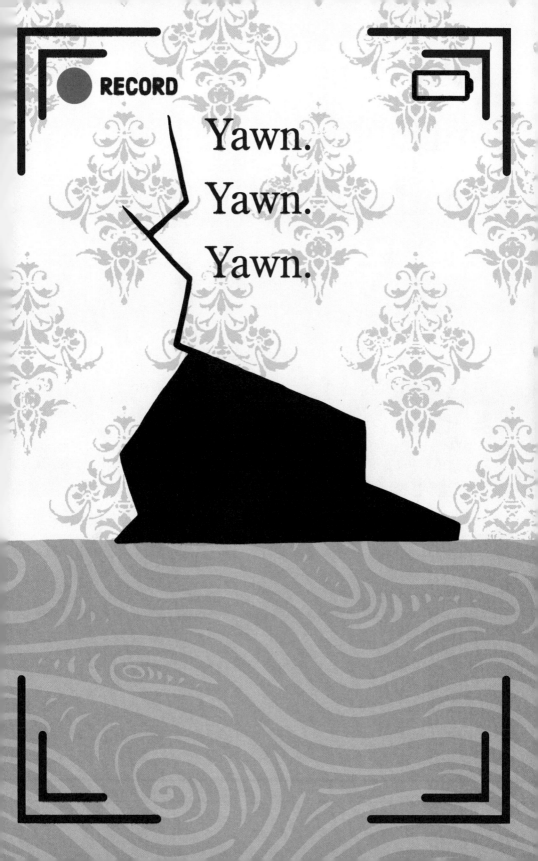

RECORD

Yawn.

Yawn.

Yawn.

Kitty-Cam . . .
FADE OUT.
Good night, Kitty.